For Aunt Londie and Uncle Mo—S. J.

With special thanks to Francine, Chris, and Amoi Ogaard—S. J.

Illustrations copyright © 1989 by Susan Jeffers. Text copyright 1941 by Artists and Writers Guild, Inc.
All rights reserved under International and Pan-American Copyright Conventions.
Published in the United States by Random House, Inc., New York,
and simultaneously in Canada by Random House of Canada Limited, Toronto.
The text was originally published in 1941 by Random House in a slightly longer version.

Library of Congress Cataloging-in-Publication Data:
Brown, Margaret Wise, 1910–1952. Baby animals / by Margaret Wise Brown ; illustrated by Susan Jeffers. p. cm.
SUMMARY: Relates the morning, noon, and evening activities of several young animals and a little girl.
ISBN: 0-394-82040-1 (trade); 0-394-92040-6 (lib. bdg.) 1. Animals—Juvenile fiction. [1. Animals—Fiction]
I. Jeffers, Susan, ill. II. Title. PZ10.3.B7656Bab 1989 [E]—dc19 88-18481

Manufactured in the United States of America 1 2 3 4 5 6 7 8 9 0

MARGARET WISE BROWN
BABY ANIMALS
ILLUSTRATED BY SUSAN JEFFERS

RANDOM HOUSE 🏠 NEW YORK

It is morning, and everything is waking up.
Birds are waking up the way birds wake up.
Pigs are waking up the way pigs wake up.
And children are waking up too.

In the early morning the little bird woke up
before anyone else was awake.
He opened his soft, bright eyes and saw the gray light
that is in the sky before the sun comes up. And then,
what would a little bird do early in the morning?

He fluttered his wings,
and then he flapped them and flew all over the sky.
And he opened his beak and chirped and sang
in the early morning.

As the sun came up, it shone on the little black horse
who was sleeping in the field with his mother.

The little horse lifted his head
when he felt the warm sun.

He stood up and shook himself,
kicked up his heels, and nudged his sleepy old mother
until she woke up.

And what do little pigs do in the morning?

The pigs in the barnyard felt the sun
on their little pink backs.
And they grunted and snorted and squealed with joy.

What would little lambs do
when they felt the warm sun shining around them?

The little lambs bounced around in the meadows
and danced the little dances of baby lambs.

"Baaaaaaa!" said their mother, who was a sheep.
"Baaaaaaa! What a beautiful day!"

And what would the old cat and her kittens do
on this sunshiny day?
The old cat purred with one eye open
as she blinked at the sunshine.
And each of her kittens opened one eye and blinked.
And one little kitten with striped fur
began to purr and purr and purrrrr.

The mother dog sniffed the morning air.
Then she began to lick her puppies
until she had bathed them all.

And then she nosed them awake and fed them
out of her own sides.
Now they stretched themselves and waved their paws.
And one little puppy barked.

All the animals were awake. The sun was up.
But the little child was still asleep.
The child heard the birds singing and the cat purring
and the pigs grunting and the puppy barking,
and she knew it was time to wake up.
"The sun is up," said the child,
"but I will pretend that I am still asleep."

But the child was smiling,
so her mother knew that she was not asleep.
Then the child got up the way a little child gets up.
Her mother took off her pajamas and washed her
and brushed her hair and put on her blue suit.
And then she had breakfast.

At noon
the sun
like a big balloon
shines
at the top of the sky.

The sun was high at the top of the sky.
You had to look straight up to see it.
"Chirp, chirp, chirp!" said the little bird.
"I am hungry. What can I find to eat?"

He looked all around with his bright black eyes
until he found a little wiggle bug.

And then he found a little seed.
And then, best of all,
he found some kernels of corn
that some children had dropped for him.

What did the little pigs have for lunch?
The little pigs had been rooting around all morning.
And when the sun was high, the farmer brought them
a big bucket of cornmeal mash, and they ate
and ate and ate and ate and ate
until the cornmeal mash was all gone.

And what did the sheep and her little lambs have
at noon? The sheep munched the green grass.
And the little lambs ate green grass too,
when they weren't kicking up their heels.

What did the cat and her kittens have for lunch?
The old cat and all her kittens had fish.
And one little kitten had a catnip mouse.

What did the little horse have to eat at noon?
At noon, when the sun was hot in the sky,
the little horse and his mother rested under a tree.
And the little horse drank milk from his mother.
And the mother munched green grass for her dinner.

What did the puppies eat at noon?
The puppies were given their first taste of meat
that noon. And they liked it right away.
They liked it so much that their fur wiggled
all over their backs as they ate.

But the child had a different lunch from any of the animals.
A child wouldn't eat wiggle bugs like a bird, would she?
No!
Would the child eat cornmeal mash like a pig?
She might. But she would not eat green grass
like a lamb, would she?
No!
The child had her own kind of lunch.
She had a bowl of noodle soup and a glass of milk.
And for dessert she had strawberry ice cream.

Night comes on
soft and still,
with shooting stars
and a whippoorwill.

As the sun went down, the little bird flew to his tree
and sang his evening song.
He closed his bright eyes, and then he tucked his head
under his wing and went to sleep.

And where would a little horse go to sleep?
The little horse lay down in the soft green grass to rest.
And the mother horse stood above him.
Soon it would be dark,
and the meadows would be blinking with fireflies.

Where did the little lambs go to sleep?
The little lambs folded their legs and lay down
in the green grass.
The father stood guard on a high hill to see
that no one came near his little lambs.
And the mother sheep stood near them.

Where did the little pigs go to sleep?
The little pigs gave one last squeal,
wiggled one last wiggle, swallowed one last swallow,
and fell asleep as close to the mother pig
as they could wiggle.

What did the old cat and her kittens do when it got dark?
The old cat blinked and the kittens blinked.
Then the old cat purred and the kittens purred.
Then the old cat fell asleep
and the kittens fell asleep, in the quiet night.

And where did the puppies go to sleep?
It was night in the corner of the kitchen.
There was a rattle of dishes and the smell of cooking.
The light was on. The mother dog watched and listened.
But not the puppies. They were asleep.
Their stomachs were as round as little rubber balls.
They had just had their supper,
and now they were asleep in their own place
by the kitchen stove.

It is nighttime.
The child is sleepy and warm in bed.
And the father comes and the mother comes,
and they say:
"Good night, sweet dreams."

Then it was the middle of the night. It was dark.
The stars were shining and the animals were asleep
and all the children were asleep.
The little bird was asleep.
The little horse was asleep.
The little lambs were asleep.
The little pigs were asleep.
The little kittens were asleep.
The little puppies were asleep.
And the little child was asleep too—
sound asleep in the night.